7:58. WE'VE GOT TWO MINUTES.

YES, "HUNTER".

CHECK SECURITY.

IT LOOKS POOR.

HOLD ON...

...YES. THEY'RE JUST STANDING AROUND.

THEY DON'T EVEN SUSPECT--

H ... H...

RUN!

YOU SAVED MY *LIFE*, HUNTER.

IF I MOVED OR TRIED TO SPEAK, THE *BLACK WIDOW* WOULD HAVE *BITTEN* ME.

TO *TAKE* ONE LIFE, AND *SAVE* ANOTHER, WITH JUST *ONE* BULLET...

NOT BAD, IF I DO SAY SO MYSELF.

I WILL *NEVER* FORGET THIS, MY FRIEND.

DON'T MENTION IT, COSSACK.

LET'S GET OUT OF HERE *ALIVE* BEFORE WE START COUNTING *DEBTS*, SHALL WE?

WHAT'S THE *TIME*, ALEX?

ALMOST TIME FOR *LUNCH*.

I'M NOT HUNGRY.

CAN YOU RUB SOME MORE *CREAM* ON MY BACK, PLEASE?

CONSIDERING THIS IS *FACTOR 25*, SABINA, YOU SEEM TO NEED A *LOT* OF TOPPING UP.

ANYONE WOULD THINK--

...BUT *WHY*? WHATEVER YASSEN'S HERE FOR, IT'S NOTHING TO DO WITH *ME*.

I HAVEN'T SEEN HIM SINCE THE DAY I STOPPED DARRIUS SAYLE...

YOU *KILLED* MY *UNCLE*. YOU'RE STILL MY *ENEMY*.

THIS *ISN'T OVER*, GREGOROVICH!

BUT THAT WAS *BEFORE* I SAW WHAT MI6 ARE *REALLY* LIKE.

NOW THEY CAN GO JUMP OFF THE *MARINA* FOR ALL I CARE.

STILL...

I *HAVE* TO KNOW WHY HE'S HERE. WHEREVER YASSEN GOES, *TROUBLE* FOLLOWS HIM.

HIS *FRIEND* DOESN'T LOOK HAPPY. BUT I'M TOO EXPOSED OUT HERE.

KLIK

EXCUSEZ-MOI, MONSIEUR!

WATCH WHERE YOU'RE GOING, YOU *IMBECILE!*

OH, GOD, LOOK AT *THAT* ONE!

*FOUR* OUT OF TWENTY, *MAX.*

THAT ONE'S *SLIGHTLY* BETTER.

MAYBE A *SIX.* AREN'T THERE *ANY* GOOD-LOOKING BOYS IN FRANCE?

*PRESENT* COMPANY EXCEPTED, OF COURSE, ALEX.

ALEX?

SORRY, I WAS *MILES* AWAY.

SO WHAT DO *I* SCORE ON YOUR FAMOUS *BOY SCALE*, THEN?

TWELVE AND A HALF. BUT *DON'T* WORRY. ANOTHER TEN YEARS AND YOU'LL BE *PERFECT.*

COME ON, LET'S GET *OUT* OF HERE.

First published 2012 by Walker Books Ltd
87 Vauxhall Walk, London SE11 5HJ

This edition published 2016

2 4 6 8 10 9 7 5 3 1

Text and illustrations © 2012 Walker Books Ltd
Based on the original novel *Eagle Strike* © 2003 Stormbreaker Productions Ltd

Anthony Horowitz has asserted his moral rights.

Trademarks © 2003 Stormbreaker Productions Ltd
Alex Rider™, Boy with Torch Logo™, AR Logo™

This book has been typeset in Wild Words and Serpentine Bold

Printed in China

British Library Cataloguing in Publication Data:
a catalogue record for this book is available
from the British Library

ISBN 978-1-4063-6635-8

www.walker.co.uk

# ALEX RIDER

ACTION
ADRENALINE
ADVENTURE

## EAGLE STRIKE

### THE GRAPHIC NOVEL

WALKER

**ANTHONY HOROWITZ**

ANTONY JOHNSTON • KANAKO • YUZURU

EXCUSEZ-MOI. I **KNOW** WHO DID THIS.

COMMENT?

THERE'S A BIG WHITE **YACHT** AT THE JETTY IN TOWN. YOU CAN'T MISS IT.

ON BOARD IS A MAN CALLED **YASSEN GREGOROVICH**. YOU MUST **ARREST** HIM BEFORE HE CAN **ESCAPE**.

AH...

WAIT HERE, PLEASE.

THEY **HAVE** TO BELIEVE ME. ALL THEY NEED TO **DO** IS CHECK OUT THE YACHT.

HELLO,

WHAT'S THAT?

Caviar for breakfast, and the swimming pool at his Wiltshire mansion is rumoured to have been built in the shape of Elvis Presley. But Damian Cray is more than the world's richest and most successful pop star. His business ventures—including hotels, TV stations and computer games—have added millions more to his personal fortune. The questions remain. Why was Cray in Paris earlier this week and why did he arrange a secret meeting with

AN "ASSASSIN" WOULD **NOT** HARM A FAMILY ON HOLIDAY. BUT YOU ARE IN SHOCK, AND DO NOT **KNOW** WHAT YOU ARE **SAYING**.

WE HAVE SENT FOR SOMEONE FROM YOUR **CONSULATE**. HE WILL ARRIVE SOON FOR YOU.

THEY DIDN'T **BELIEVE** ME. I SHOULD HAVE **KNOWN**!

IT'S ONLY A **MILE** TO SAINT-PIERRE. I **HAVE** TO REACH THE BOAT BEFORE YASSEN **LEAVES**...

...I HAVE TO **MAKE UP** FOR MY OWN **STUPIDITY**.

WHAK!

UNH!

HE MUST HAVE BEEN SITTING *HERE* BEFORE HE WENT OUT ON THE JETTY.

THAT *PHONE* LOOKS FAMILIAR.

IT'S THE ONE *YASSEN* USED IN THE RESTAURANT. LET'S SEE *WHO* HE WAS CALLING...

12:53
44-207-79460909

*44* IS THE CODE FOR ENGLAND. AND *207* IS LONDON.

THIS IS THE NUMBER OF WHOEVER GAVE THE *ORDER!*

GIVE THE BRAT TO *ME*. I WILL KILL HIM *MYSELF* AND THROW HIM OVERBOARD FOR THE *FISH*.

IT'S LUCKY THAT RAOUL CAME BACK FROM TOWN WHEN HE *DID*, FRANCO.

YOU WERE *SUPPOSED* TO BE GUARDING THE BOAT.

HOW DID HE *FIND* US? HOW DOES HE KNOW WHO WE *ARE*?

A GOOD QUESTION. REMEMBER, ALEX, YOU ARE ALIVE ONLY BECAUSE *I* PERMIT IT. SO TELL ME, ARE YOU HERE WITH *MI6*?

NO. I'M ON *HOLIDAY*, AND I SAW THE YACHT COME IN. I SAW *YOU*.

AND YOU FOLLOWED US TO THE RESTAURANT?

YES.

I *THOUGHT* THERE WAS SOMEONE... YOU WERE STAYING IN THE *VILLA*?

I WAS INVITED BY A FRIEND.

HER FATHER'S A *JOURNALIST*. WAS *HE* THE ONE YOU WERE HIRED TO KILL?

THAT IS *NONE* OF YOUR BUSINESS. IT WAS *BAD LUCK* YOU WERE THERE, ALEX. NOTHING PERSONAL.

SURE. WITH YOU IT NEVER *IS*.

WHAT DO WE *DO* WITH HIM?

JUST LET *ME* DEAL WITH HIM! HE'LL NEVER TALK *AGAIN!*

I DO *NOT* KILL CHILDREN. THE BOY KNOWS NOTHING. BUT WE *CANNOT* JUST LET HIM GO.

YOU DID *NOT* KILL ME WHEN YOU HAD A CHANCE, ALEX. SO I WILL GIVE *YOU* A CHANCE, TOO.

YOU HAVE *COURAGE*. NOW YOU MUST *DISPLAY* IT.

**KRAKA-THOOM!!**

HMMM. THAT NUMBER I FOUND ON YASSEN'S MOBILE...

YASSEN WILL BE LONG GONE. SO *NOW* WHAT?

OPERATOR?

A REVERSE CHARGE CALL TO *ENGLAND*, PLEASE. THE NUMBER IS *4420779460909*.

MY NAME?

JUST ... JUST SAY *YASSEN GREGOROVIC* IS CALLING.

THEY PROBABLY WON'T EVEN *ANSWER*. IT'S LATE IN ENGLAND, TOO.

YOUR CALL HAS BEEN ACCEPTED, MONSIEUR. ONE MOMENT...

*OH!* THANK YOU.

*DAMIAN CRAY* SPEAKING.

HELLO?

WHO'S THERE? IS THIS SOME KIND OF *JOKE*?

KLIK!

ONLY *THREE* BOOKS ABOUT ONE OF THE MOST *FAMOUS* MEN IN THE WORLD?!

THESE TWO BARELY *QUALIFY* AS BOOKS, THEY'RE JUST PUFF PIECES FULL OF GLOSSY PICTURES.

AND THIS ONE LOOKS LIKE IT WAS WRITTEN BY SOMEONE WHO READS THE *FINANCIAL TIMES* FOR *LAUGHS*.

NONE OF THEM WILL TELL ME ANYTHING *NEW*. WHAT I NEED TO KNOW IS WHY DAMIAN CRAY'S NUMBER WAS ON *YASSEN'S* MOBILE!

OH, WELL. HOME, I GUESS.

YOU CAN'T BLAME *YOURSELF*. LIKE YOU SAID, YOU DIDN'T *KNOW* WHAT WOULD HAPPEN.

BESIDES, YOU *TRIED* TO TELL THE POLICE AND THEY DIDN'T BELIEVE YOU.

GOING AFTER THIS YASSEN GUY ON YOUR *OWN* WAS TOO DANGEROUS, THOUGH. YOU COULD HAVE BEEN *KILLED*!

I HAD TO DO *SOMETHING*.

*LISTEN* TO ME, ALEX. YES, YOUR UNCLE IAN WAS A *SPY*. YES, HE HAD SOME CRAZY IDEA ABOUT *TRAINING* YOU.

BUT YOU'RE *NOT* A SPY.

*THREE* TIMES NOW THEY'VE DRAGGED YOU OUT OF SCHOOL, AND EVERY TIME YOU COME BACK *MORE* BASHED AROUND THAN THE LAST. I'VE BEEN WORRIED *SICK*!

BUT IT WASN'T MY *CHOICE*...

*EXACTLY*. SPIES AND BULLETS AND MADMEN HAVE GOT *NOTHING* TO DO WITH YOU. YOU WERE RIGHT TO WALK AWAY.

HAROLD **LEFT** THE ACADEMY TO TRAVEL THE WORLD.

HE CHANGED HIS **NAME**, BECAME A **BUDDHIST** AND A **VEGETARIAN** FOR A WHILE ... DID YOU KNOW ALL HIS CONCERT TICKETS ARE MADE FROM **RECYCLED PAPER?**

HE CAME BACK TO ENGLAND AND FORMED THE BAND **SLAM!**, WHO WERE AN INSTANT SUCCESS.

WHEN THEY SPLIT UP, CRAY BEGAN A **SOLO** CAREER.

HIS FIRST ALBUM WENT **PLATINUM**, AND FOR A WHILE HE WAS SELDOM OUT OF THE TOP TWENTY.

HE WON FIVE **GRAMMYS** AND AN **ACADEMY AWARD.**

THEN, IN THE '80S, HE VISITED **AFRICA** DURING THE FAMINE.

WHEN HE CAME BACK HE STAGED **CHART ATTACK**, AN ENORMOUS CONCERT AT WEMBLEY, AND A CHRISTMAS SINGLE THAT SOLD **FOUR MILLION** COPIES.

HE GAVE EVERY PENNY OF THE PROFITS TO **CHARITY.**

HE BOUGHT A *TV STATION*, THEN A CHAIN OF *HOTELS*, AND HIS LATEST THING IS *VIDEOGAMES*.

HE'S ABOUT TO LAUNCH A NEW CONSOLE CALLED *"GAMESLAYER"* THAT WILL APPARENTLY PUT THE OTHERS IN THE SHADE.

HE HAS *ENORMOUS* INFLUENCE. LAST ELECTION, HE DONATED A *MILLION POUNDS* TO THE GOVERNMENT.

IF IT WAS *DISCOVERED* WE WERE INVESTIGATING HIM ON THE WORD OF A *SCHOOLBOY*, IT WOULD BE A *SCANDAL!*

THE *PRIME MINISTER* DOESN'T LIKE US *ANYWAY*. HE COULD USE AN ATTACK ON CRAY TO SHUT US DOWN.

HEATHROW LIVE

BBC

CRAY WAS ON TV *TODAY*, TOO. THIS IS FROM THIS MORNING...

HEATHROW LIVE

...PRESIDENT OF THE *UNITED STATES* ARRIVED TODAY IN *AIR FORCE ONE*, THE PRESIDENTIAL PLANE, AND IS DUE TO HAVE LUNCH WITH THE *PRIME MINISTER* AT DOWNING STREET TODAY.

HEATHROW LIVE

...BUT *FIRST* HE MET FORMER POP SINGER, NOW CAMPAIGNER FOR ENVIRONMENTAL AND POLITICAL ISSUES, *DAMIAN CRAY.*

BBC

THEY DISCUSSED **GREENPEACE'S** EFFORTS TO STOP ALASKAN OIL DRILLING, AND ALTHOUGH HE MADE NO PROMISES, THE PRESIDENT AGREED TO **READ** THE REPORT...

LIVE

DO YOU SEE? THE MOST **POWERFUL** MAN IN THE WORLD INTERRUPTS HIS HOLIDAY TO MEET DAMIAN CRAY-- **BEFORE** THE PRIME MINISTER!

SO TELL ME, WHAT **POSSIBLE** REASON WOULD A MAN LIKE THAT HAVE TO BLOW UP A VILLA, AND PERHAPS **KILL** A FAMILY?

THAT'S WHAT I WANT YOU TO **FIND OUT!**

WELL, WE'RE GOING TO **WAIT** UNTIL THE FRENCH POLICE GET BACK TO US.

THEY'RE INVESTIGATING THESE **"CST"** TERRORISTS.

SO YOU'RE GOING TO DO *NOTHING!*

I THINK WE HAVE EXPLAINED SUFFICIENTLY, ALEX.

YOU KNOW, IT'S AMAZING. WHEN YOU NEED *ME*, YOU JUST *PULL* ME OUT OF SCHOOL AND SEND ME HALFWAY ACROSS THE WORLD.

BUT WHEN I NEED *YOU*, JUST THIS ONCE, YOU WON'T DO A *THING!*

CRAY *MIGHT* BE FATHER CHRISTMAS, JOAN OF ARC AND THE POPE ALL ROLLED INTO ONE, BUT IT *WAS* HIS VOICE I HEARD ON THE PHONE!

I KNOW HE'S INVOLVED SOMEHOW. AND I'LL *PROVE* IT TO YOU!

WELL?

I'LL GO OVER THE *FILES* AGAIN. AFTER ALL, *DARRIUS SAYLE* PRETENDED TO BE A FRIEND OF THE BRITISH PEOPLE, AND IF NOT FOR ALEX...

CURIOUS THAT HE SHOULD RUN INTO *YASSEN* AGAIN, WOULDN'T YOU SAY?

YES. AND THAT YASSEN DIDN'T *KILL* ALEX WHEN HE HAD THE CHANCE.

I WOULDN'T SAY *THAT*, ALL THINGS CONSIDERED.

MAYBE WE SHOULD TELL HIM...

ABSOLUTELY NOT.

THE *LESS* ALEX RIDER KNOWS ABOUT YASSEN GREGOROVICH, THE *BETTER*.

TODAY IS A GREAT OCCASION!

UNLESS YOU'RE FROM *SONY* OR *MICROSOFT*, THAT IS. SORRY GUYS, BUT YOU'RE *HISTORY*.

HA HA HA HA HA

MR CRAY ... THE FIRST GAME IS A *SHOOTER*, ISN'T IT? AS A *PEACE CAMPAIGNER*, HOW CAN YOU *JUSTIFY* SELLING VIOLENT GAMES TO CHILDREN?

WELL, WE *DID* DEVELOP A GAME WHERE THE HERO COLLECTED *FLOWERS* AND PUT THEM IN A *VASE*.

STRANGELY, *NONE* OF OUR GAME TESTERS WANTED TO PLAY IT!

HA HA HA HA

BUT SERIOUSLY, MODERN KIDS HAVE A LOT OF *AGGRESSIO* IT'S HUMAN NATURE.

I THINK IT'S BETTER FOR THEM TO RELEASE IT PLAYING *GAMES* THAN OU ON THE *STREET*.

BUT YOU'RE STILL ENCOURAGING **VIOLENCE**!

I'VE **ANSWERED** YOUR QUESTION, SO MAYBE YOU SHOULD STOP **QUESTIONING** MY ANSWER.

CLAP CLAP CLAP CLAP

**GAMESLAYER** HAS GRAPHICS LIKE NO OTHER SYSTEM. IT CAN GENERATE WORLDS, CHARACTERS AND COMPLEX PHYSICAL SIMULATIONS.

GAMESLAYER

OTHER SYSTEMS GIVE YOU **PLASTIC DOLLS**. WITH GAMESLAYER, HAIR, EYES, WATER, SMOKE ... EVERYTHING LOOKS LIKE THE **REAL THING**.

WE OBEY THE RULES OF GRAVITY AND FRICTION. AND WE'VE BUILT SOMETHING CALLED **PAIN SYNTHESIS**.

THE BEST WAY TO SHOW YOU IS TO **PLAY**. IT. DO WE HAVE ANY **TEENAGERS** IN THE AUDIENCE?

**HERE'S ONE!**

WHAT? NO, WAIT...

EXCELLENT! GIVE OUR VOLUNTEER A BIG HAND!

CLAP CLAP CLAP CLAP CLAP

WHAT'S YOUR NAME?

ALEX RIDER.

PLEASED TO MEET YOU, ALEX RIDER. I'M DAMIAN CRAY ... AND YOU'RE GOING TO BE THE *FIRST* PERSON TO PLAY OUR FIRST GAME, *FEATHERED SERPENT!*

CLAP CLAP CLAP CLAP

IT'S BASED ON THE *AZTEC* CIVILIZATION. SOME CLAIM THE AZTECS CAME TO MEXICO FROM *ANOTHER PLANET.* AND THAT'S WHERE ALEX IS, ON A MISSION TO FIND FOUR MISSING SUNS!

BUT FIRST HE MUST ENTER THE TEMPLE OF *TLALOC*, FIGHT HIS WAY THROUGH THE CHAMBERS, AND THROW HIMSELF INTO THE *POOL OF FIRE* TO ADVANCE TO THE NEXT LEVEL.

PSST!

TRY LOOKING BEHIND THE IVY!!

HA HA HA HA

WELL, THIS SHOULD BE EASY...

BZZZZT!

AAAH!

AAAH!

OH, SORRY. DIDN'T I TELL YOU IT WAS *ELECTRIFIED*?

HAHA HAHA

CRAY *TRICKED* ME INTO TOUCHING THE IVY DELIBERATELY. WELL, THAT DOES IT. I'M *NOT* GOING TO LOSE TO HIS STUPID GAME!

SQUAAAAWK!

HSSSSS!

HA HA HA HA

YOU'RE MAKING IT LOOK TOO *EASY!*

SQUAAWK!

BUMP

HEY...!

**AAAAIIIEEEE!**

SORRY, ALEX. GUESS IT *WASN'T* AS EASY AS YOU *THOUGHT!*

BUT YOU DID GREAT. GIVE YOUR *NAME* TO ONE OF MY ASSISTANTS AND I'LL SEND YOU A *FREE* GAMESLAYER!

AT LEAST NOW I KNOW *ONE* THING FOR SURE.

WHETHER OR NOT HE HIRED YASSEN TO PLANT THE *BOMB*, DAMIAN CRAY IS A ROTTEN *CHEAT!*

**LATER:**

...TODAY'S BIG LAUNCH OF THE NEW *GAMESLAYER* CONSOLE FROM SIR DAMIAN CRAY'S COMPANY *CST* WAS AN ENORMOUS SUCCESS, ACCORDING TO INDUSTRY EXPERTS...

DON'T FEEL BAD. A *LOT* OF RICH MEN ARE SORE LOSERS, AND CRAY IS *VERY* RICH.

BUT DOES IT *PROVE* ANYTHING?

I DON'T KNOW. MAYBE WE SHOULD GO TO *PARIS* AND TRY TO FIND THAT PHOTOGRAPHER, *MARC ANTONIO.*

WITH A NAME LIKE *THAT* HE SHOULDN'T BE TOO HARD TO LOCATE. AND I DO *LOVE* PARIS.

I STILL DON'T HAVE ANY *PROOF*, THOUGH. IT MIGHT BE A WASTE OF TIME.

AND NOW THAT I'VE MET CRAY ... I DON'T *LIKE* HIM, BUT HE'S AN ENTERTAINER. A *BUSINESSMAN.* HE DIDN'T LOOK LIKE THE SORT OF MAN WHO'D *HURT* ANYONE.

BONJOUR. CAN I SPEAK TO **MARC ANTONIO**, PLEASE?

HE IS NOT HERE. WHO ARE **YOU**?

MY NAME IS ALEX RIDER, AND I'M A FRIEND OF **EDWARD PLEASURE**. HE'S A JOURNALIST--

I **KNOW** WHO HE IS.

THEN YOU PROBABLY **ALSO** KNOW WHAT HAPPENED TO HIM.

I **MUST** SPEAK TO MARC ANTONIO. IT'S ABOUT **DAMIAN CRAY**.

*LA PALETTE*. IT IS A **CAFÉ** ON THE RUE DE SEINE. ONE O'CLOCK.

KLIK!

I HAVEN'T BEEN TO PARIS IN **YEARS**. I THOUGHT IF I CAME BACK IT WOULD BE TO STUDY **ART**, NOT CALL ROUND PHOTO AGENCIES AND ARRANGE SHADY **MEETINGS** WITH GUYS I DON'T KNOW.

DON'T BE LIKE THAT, JACK. WHERE'S YOUR SENSE OF **ADVENTURE**?

THIS WAY.

C'EST LUI QUI A *TÉLÉPHONÉ*?

OUI.

YOU MUST BE MARC ANTONIO.

YES.

BUT YOU SAY YOU ARE EDWARD PLEASURE'S *FRIEND*? I DIDN'T KNOW HE HUNG OUT WITH *KIDS*.

I KNOW HIS *DAUGHTER*. I WAS STAYING WITH THEM, WHEN...

YOU KNOW WHAT *HAPPENED* TO HIM?

MOVE!

UP IS THE ONLY WAY!

KEEP GOING! I CAN HEAR THEM *BELOW* US!

ONTO THE ROOF! QUICK--

AAAAARGH!

LATER:

ARE THEY *INSANE*? IF THERE'S ANY *FUEL* IN THERE, IT'LL *EXPLODE*!

...HUH?

THE PLANE'S NOT EVEN *DAMAGED*. BUT WHAT DOES THIS HAVE TO DO WITH *VIDEO GAMES*?

THEY WENT IN *THIS CUBE* ... SO WHERE ARE THEY NOW?

A-HA. DOWN THERE.

I'M VERY GRATEFUL, **MR ROPER.** THANKS TO YOU, **EAGLE STRIKE** WILL PROCEED ON SCHEDULE.

I'VE ENJOYED DOING **BUSINESS** WITH YOU, MR CRAY.

YOU SAY THE **GOLD CODES** CHANGE DAILY. PRESUMABLY THIS DRIVE IS PROGRAMMED WITH TODAY'S. BUT WHAT IF EAGLE STRIKE TAKES PLACE **TOMORROW**?

JUST PLUG IT IN AND THE FLASH DRIVE **UPDATES** ITSELF. THE ONLY PROBLEM, LIKE I TOLD YOU, IS THE SMALL MATTER OF THE **FINGER** ON THE **BUTTON.**

WE'VE ALREADY **SOLVED** THAT. JUST ONE MORE THING. HOW CAN I BE **SURE** THE DRIVE WILL WORK?

YOU HAVE MY **WORD.** AND YOU'RE CERTAINLY **PAYING** ME ENOUGH.

TRUE. **HALF** A MILLION DOLLARS IN ADVANCE, AND **TWO** MILLION NOW. HOWEVER, I DO STILL HAVE ONE SMALL WORRY.

WHAT'S THE PROBLEM?

HENRYK, ADRIAAN, LEAVE US.

YASSEN *TOLD* ME ABOUT YOU, ALEX. APPARENTLY YOU ONCE WORKED FOR MI6. HOW *NOVEL*! DID THEY SEND YOU?

MI6 KNOW *NOTHING*. EVEN IF THEY DID, THEY WOULDN'T SEND *ALEX*.

THEN WHY WAS HE AT THE *PLEASURE DOME*? WHY IS HE HERE? I *DOUBT* HE WANTS MY AUTOGRAPH.

YOU COMPLETELY *SPOILT* MY GAMESLAYER LAUNCH, ALEX. I WAS PLANNING A LITTLE *ACCIDENT* FOR YOU.

LIKE YOU DID FOR THAT JOURNALIST, SUSAN WRIGHT?

I HATE *JOURNALISTS* ALMOST AS MUCH AS I HATE *SMART-ARSED KIDS*.

BUT I'M *GLAD* YOU'RE HERE. YOU'VE MADE THINGS *MUCH* EASIER.

MI6 *KNOW* I'M HERE, AND ABOUT EAGLE STRIKE. YOU MAY *HAVE* THE CODES, BUT YOU'LL NEVER BE ABLE TO *USE* THEM.

IF I DON'T REPORT BACK BY THIS EVENING, THIS PLACE WILL BE *SURROUNDED*.

KLIK

I WISH I'D PAID MORE **ATTENTION** TO THE GAME, NOW. THERE WAS A **CROSSBOW**, BEHIND THE ELECTRIFIED IVY...

W°°°°S4

WHAT THE--?

Aah!

CHNG!

DON'T FORGET THE **BOOMERANG**, ALEX! **HAHA!**

THAT WAS TOO CLOSE! BUT IT HIT THE IVY AND **SHORT-CIRCUITED** IT. LUCKY BREAK!

THE CROSSBOW'S **REAL**, BUT THIS BOLT IS **BLUNT.** STILL, I MIGHT AS WELL TAKE IT.

NOW FOR THE SWORD... NO, *WAIT!*

THERE WAS ANOTHER *BOOMERANG.*

CRAY EXPECTS ME TO DO EVERYTHING JUST LIKE IN THE *GAME.* BUT I'M *NOT* A COMPUTER AVATAR! I'M A HUMAN BEING...

...AND I CAN *CHEAT!*

THIS IS THE CHAMBER WHERE THE *FLYING CREATURE* ATTACKED.

THERE, A *MODEL* UP IN THE RAFTERS! AND IT'S ON A *WIRE,* WAITING TILL I'M HALFWAY ACROSS.

WELL, NOT FOR LONG.

SNAP!

WHAT WAS NEXT?

OH, THE CORRIDOR OF **SPEARS**. AND **ACID**. GREAT.

CHOK CHOK

YEAH, THAT'S WHAT I THOUGHT.

THIS BROKEN **SPEAR TIP** WILL FIT THE CROSSBOW, THOUGH. MAYBE THINGS ARE LOOKING **UP** AFTER ALL.

"UP"!

THAT'S IT!

BUT CRUEL OR NOT, IT'S STILL *DEADLY!* IT'LL *KILL* ME IF I DON'T ACT FAST!

KTUNG!!!

TO *HELL* WITH THIS, AND TO HELL WITH *CRAY!* THIS HAS GONE FAR *ENOUGH!*

NO *CAMERAS* AROUND HERE. BUT THE ONLY EXIT LEADS TO THE GODS, WHERE I *DIED* IN THE GAME.

HMMMMM.

GOOD JOB THEY DIDN'T LOOK TOO *CLOSELY*! BUT THE *SNAKE'S BLOOD* WAS PRETTY CONVINCING, AND THAT WIRE *WAS* USEFUL AFTER ALL.

NOW TO FIND A WAY *OUT* OF THE COMPOUND, AND FAST, BEFORE THEY REALIZE I'VE GONE!

BETTER FIND SOMETHING TO *WEAR*, THOUGH. I'LL *FREEZE* OUTSIDE OTHERWISE.

*TWO HOURS* SINCE I GOT HERE. JACK WILL BE GOING *SPARE* BACK AT THE HOTEL!

NOBODY AROUND. ALL OF CRAY'S SECURITY IS FOCUSED ON KEEPING PEOPLE *OUT*, NOT IN.

THERE'S THE *FLASH DRIVE!* MI6 WILL *HAVE* TO BELIEVE ME NOW!

NOBODY HERE IN CRAY'S *LOUNGE*, EITHER.

TIME TO GO. GOT TO GET BACK TO *LONDON* AS QUICKLY AS POSSIBLE.

THEY TOLD ME HE WAS *DEAD!* AND NOW HE'S *STOLEN* THE FLASH DRIVE!

YOU *KNEW* HE'D COME IN HERE!

I SUSPECTED IT. HE IS *ALEX*, AFTER ALL.

WHO *IS* THIS BOY? *TELL* ME ABOUT HIM!

THERE IS NO OTHER BOY *LIKE* HIM. CONSIDER: TONIGHT YOU TRIED TO *KILL* HIM, IN A MANNER THAT SHOULD HAVE *TERRIFIED* HIM.

AND WHEN MOST BOYS – MOST *MEN*, EVEN – WOULD HAVE RUN STRAIGHT FOR THE STAIRS, HE DID *NOT*.

BUT NOT ONLY DID HE *SURVIVE*, HE ALSO *ESCAPED*.

HE STOPPED AND SEARCHED. HE CARRIED OUT HIS *OBJECTIVE*.

I'M *EXHAUSTED.* GLAD I LEFT THE *BIKE* HERE AT THE STATION, SO I DON'T HAVE TO WALK TO THE HOTEL.

A PLANE ON *FIRE,* SECRET CODES WORTH TWO AND A HALF MILLION DOLLARS, THE *NSA,* A VIP ROOM ... WHAT DOES IT ALL *MEAN?*

AMSTERDAM, HOLLAND

AND I STILL HAVE NO IDEA WHAT *"EAGLE STRIKE"* IS--

EH?

THOSE *CARS* AREN'T PARKED NORMALLY. AND THEY ALL SEEM TO BE FACING *ME...*

UH-OH.

I HAVE MEN WATCHING *EVERY* STATION AND AIRPORT IN HOLLAND. BUT I THINK ALEX WILL HEAD FOR *PARIS*, OR *BRUSSELS*, AND FROM THERE TO ENGLAND.

I'M *VERY* DISAPPOINTED, MR GREGOROVICH. I WAS TOLD YOU WERE THE *BEST*. THAT YOU *NEVER* MAKE MISTAKES.

BUT NOW IT'S ALL OVER! EAGLE STRIKE WILL *NEVER* HAPPEN!

IT'S *NOT* OVER. I HAVE PEOPLE IN ENGLAND. WE *WILL* GET THE FLASH DRIVE BACK.

HOW?!

*WHY* WAS ALEX IN FRANCE? *WHY* DID HE CARE ABOUT THIS JOURNALIST? HE RISKED HIS LIFE FOR THIS MAN.

IT IS BECAUSE OF HIS *DAUGHTER. THAT* IS WHO ALEX WAS STAYING WITH.

A *GIRLFRIEND...*

OH, YES. *YES*, THAT SHOULD BE VERY USEFUL *INDEED*.

CHELSEA, LONDON

WE **HAVE** TO GO TO MI6.

**NO!** YOU HEARD WHAT HE SAID. BESIDES, MI6 WOULDN'T BE ABLE TO DO **ANYTHING** BEFORE CRAY'S **DEADLINE**.

SABINA IS ONLY IN THIS MESS BECAUSE OF **ME**. I **CAN'T** LET HER DIE.

A LOT **MORE** PEOPLE COULD DIE IF EAGLE STRIKE GOES AHEAD.

WE DON'T **KNOW** THAT. WE DON'T EVEN KNOW WHAT EAGLE STRIKE **IS**!

YOU THINK HE'D GO TO ALL THIS TROUBLE JUST TO ROB A **BANK**? ALEX, HE'S A **KILLER**!

ALL RIGHT. I THINK I KNOW **HOW** I CAN DO THIS, BUT I HAVE TO GO **ALONE**. YOU STAY HERE AND CONTACT MI6, JUST IN CASE.

AND IF IT **DOESN'T** WORK?

THEN CRAY WINS, AND EAGLE STRIKE HAPPENS.

WHATEVER IT ACTUALLY IS.

"I HATED EVERY **SECOND** OF THE ROYAL ACADEMY. BACH, BEETHOVEN, MOZART ... I WAS A **TEENAGER**! I WANTED TO BE ELVIS PRESLEY, TO BE **FAMOUS**!

"MY FATHER WAS **MOST** UPSET. THEY THOUGHT I'D SING **OPERA** AT COVENT GARDEN, OR SOMETHING GHASTLY LIKE THAT, AND **REFUSED** TO LET ME LEAVE.

"BUT THEN THEY HAD THAT TERRIBLE **ACCIDENT**. I **PRETENDED** TO BE VERY UPSET, BUT I WASN'T. AND I REALIZED THAT GOD WAS ON **MY** SIDE! HE **WANTED** ME TO BE FAMOUS!

"ANYWAY, I **INHERITED** ALL THEIR MONEY. I BOUGHT A PENTHOUSE IN LONDON, AND SET UP A BAND CALLED **SLAM**!

"THE REST IS **HISTORY**. SOON I WAS THE GREATEST SINGER IN THE **WORLD**.

"AND **THAT** WAS WHEN I STARTED TO THINK **ABOUT** THE WORLD I WAS IN.

"ALL MY LIFE I'VE WANTED TO **HELP** PEOPLE. YOU THINK I'M A **MONSTER**, ALEX, BUT I'VE RAISED **MILLIONS** FOR CHARITY. THE QUEEN HERSELF **KNIGHTED** ME FOR IT!

"BUT SOMETIMES THAT'S NOT **ENOUGH**. I COULD RAISE MONEY, BUT I COULDN'T GET PEOPLE TO **LISTEN** TO ME.

"TAKE THE CASE OF THE **MILBURN INSTITUTE**.

"THIS WAS A LABORATORY THAT TESTED **COSMETICS** ON ANIMALS, FOR MANY DIFFERENT COMPANIES.

"I CAMPAIGNED FOR OVER A **YEAR** TO GET THEM SHUT DOWN. WE HAD A PETITION WITH **TWENTY THOUSAND** SIGNATURES. BUT THEY WOULDN'T LISTEN.

"SO I HAD PROFESSOR MILBURN **KILLED**.

"**VOILÀ!** SIX MONTHS LATER THE INSTITUTE CLOSED DOWN. END OF STORY. **NO** MORE ANIMALS HARMED.

"I HAD A LOT **MORE** PEOPLE KILLED AFTER THAT.

"THERE WAS A CORPORATION CUTTING DOWN **RAINFORESTS** IN BRAZIL. I HAD THEM KILLED AND BURIED IN THE JUNGLE. AND SOME JAPANESE **WHALERS**, LOCKED IN THEIR OWN DEEP FREEZE..."

I **HATED** HAVING TO BLOW UP YOUR FATHER. IF HE HADN'T SPIED ON ME, I WOULDN'T HAVE **HAD** TO. BUT I **COULDN'T** LET HIM SPOIL MY PLANS.

THIS IS A **TERRIBLE** WORLD, AND IF YOU WANT TO MAKE A DIFFERENCE, SOMETIMES YOU HAVE TO BE A BIT **EXTREME**.

AND THAT'S THAT.

I HAVE A COUPLE OF **QUESTIONS**.

OF COURSE. GO ON.

YASSEN, **WHY** ARE YOU WORKING FOR THIS **LUNATIC?**

ALL MY LIFE I'VE **FOUGHT** DRUGS. ADVERTS FOR THE GOVERNMENT, BUILDING TREATMENT CENTRES, WRITING ALBUMS ABOUT HOW **EVIL** THEY ARE.

BUT NOW I'M GOING TO **END** IT. THAT'S WHAT EAGLE STRIKE IS. IMAGINE A WORLD **WITHOUT** DRUGS! ISN'T THAT **WORTH** A FEW SACRIFICES?

HOW?

EASY. **GOVERNMENTS** WON'T DO ANYTHING. THE **POLICE** ARE POWERLESS. **NO-ONE** CAN STOP THE DEALERS. SO YOU HAVE TO GO TO THE **SUPPLIERS**.

AFGHANISTAN, BURMA, PAKISTAN, COLOMBIA, CHINA, ALBANIA, PERU ... THOUSANDS OF TONS OF **HEROIN, COCAINE** AND **MARIJUANA** PRODUCED EVERY YEAR, AND SOLD ALL OVER THE **WORLD!**

**THESE** ARE THE PRINCIPAL SOURCES OF THE WORLD'S DRUG PROBLEM.

THESE ARE MY **TARGETS**.

VRRRRRM...

WE'RE HERE!
*EVERYBODY OUT!*

WE'RE RIGHT NEXT TO THE *AIRPORT.* WHAT'S CRAY UP TO?

TURN ON THE *SPEAKER,* HENRYK!

*SSSSSSZZZKKK*

ATTENTION, AIR TRAFFIC CONTROL. THIS IS *MILLENNIUM AIR* FLIGHT 118 FROM *AMSTERDAM.* WE HAVE A *PROBLEM.*

RIGHT ON TIME!

SOMETHING ABOUT THAT PLANE LOOKS *FAMILIAR...*

ROGER, *MA118.* WHAT IS YOUR PROBLEM, OVER?

I DON'T UNDERSTAND. WHAT'S HE *DOING?*

THE PLANE ISN'T *REALLY* ON FIRE. HE'S USING IT TO *EVACUATE* THE AIRPORT, SO WE CAN GET *IN.*

*ENOUGH.* YOU DO NOT TALK, NOW. PUT YOUR HOODS UP AND WEAR *THESE.*

WHY?

JUST DO AS I *SAY.*

*HMPH!* WELL, IT'LL *RUIN* MY MAKE-UP.

THE MASKS MAKE US *ANONYMOUS.* THE AIRPORT IS EXPECTING A *HAZMAT TEAM,* AND THAT'S WHAT WE *LOOK* LIKE.

WOOOOOO WOOOOO

IT *WORKED!* THE GUARDS DIDN'T EVEN *CHECK* OUR ID. THEY JUST WANT THIS *DEALT* WITH AS SOON AS POSSIBLE!

WHY IS HE STEALING THE PRESIDENT'S *PLANE?*

AIR FORCE ONE IS A MOBILE *COMMAND CENTRE.* *ANYTHING* YOU CAN DO IN THE WHITE HOUSE, YOU CAN DO FROM THIS PLANE...

...INCLUDING STARTING A *NUCLEAR WAR.*

ALL CLEAR!

THEN LET'S GET ON *BOARD.* YOU TOO, HENRYK!

THE SOLDIERS ARE WEARING AMERICAN *UNIFORMS* UNDERNEATH. ANYONE LOOKING WILL THINK IT'S BUSINESS AS *USUAL!*

WELCOME ON BOARD, ALEX. *IMPRESSIVE,* ISN'T IT?

DO HURRY UP AND STASH THOSE *BODIES* SOMEWHERE, MR GREGOROVICH. THEY'RE *RUINING* THE MOMENT.

ALEX, COME WITH ME. I WANT YOU TO *WATCH*.

*YOU* STAY HERE WITH MR GREGOROVICH, YOUNG LADY. DON'T TRY ANYTHING *SILLY*.

UP HERE. IT'S NOT FAR.

THE **COMMUNICATIONS CENTRE** OF AIR FORCE ONE. AND WE HAVE IT ALL TO **OURSELVES.**

THIS IS THE **MOMENT OF TRUTH,** ALEX. I'M SO GLAD YOU BROUGHT THE FLASH DRIVE BACK.

BUT PLEASE, **DON'T** MOVE. I WANT YOU TO SEE THIS, BUT IF YOU EVEN **BLINK** I'LL **SHOOT** YOU.

THESE COMPUTERS ARE LINKED TO **MOUNT CHEYENNE,** A SECRET UNDERGROUND **CONTROL CENTRE** FOR AMERICA'S NUCLEAR WEAPONS.

THE LAUNCH CODES FOR THE MISSILES ARE **CHANGED** EVERY DAY AND SENT TO THE PRESIDENT BY THE NSA. A SATELLITE CALLED **MILSTAR** SENDS TWO COPIES.

ONE GOES TO THE **PENTAGON,** AND THE OTHER ONE...

WELL, THAT'S THAT. IN *NINETY MINUTES* THE MISSILES WILL HIT THEIR *TARGETS.*

*NO!* WHEN THEY REALIZE WHAT'S HAPPENED, SOMEONE WILL MAKE THE MISSILES *SELF-DESTRUCT!*

IT'S NOT THAT *EASY.* IT WAS THE AIR FORCE ONE COMPUTER THAT ORDERED THE LAUNCH, SO *ONLY* AIR FORCE ONE CAN *TERMINATE* THEM.

AND I *SAW* YOU EYEING THAT SELF-DESTRUCT BUTTON, BUT YOU'RE NOT GETTING ANYWHERE *NEAR* IT. WE'RE LEAVING.

WE'RE READY, HENRYK. PREPARE FOR *TAKEOFF.*

ONCE THIS PLANE IS *AIRBORNE,* IT'S VIRTUALLY *INDESTRUCTIBLE.* A PERFECT GETAWAY VEHICLE!

AND EVEN IF THEY *DO* SHOOT US DOWN, THE MISSILES WILL LAND. THE WORLD WILL *STILL* BE *SAVED!*

HE'S RIGHT. IF I'M GOING TO STOP THIS SOMEHOW, IT HAS TO BE *BEFORE* WE TAKE OFF!

UHHH...

SABINA ... I CAN'T MOVE MY LEGS...

YOU HAVE TO GET TO THE **COMMUNICATIONS ROOM.** SELF-DESTRUCT BUTTON ... THE **MISSILES**...

OK...

YES, OF COURSE...

ALEX.

YASSEN?

I THOUGHT YOU WERE *DEAD*...

NOT ... YET.

WHAT HAPPENED ... TO CRAY?

HE WENT OFF HIS TROLLEY. *DEAD*, I MEAN.

GOOD.

I KNEW IT WAS ... A *MISTAKE* WORKING FOR HIM.

THERE IS SOMETHING ... I *MUST* TELL YOU. I COULDN'T ... KILL YOU, ALEX. I NEVER WOULD. BECAUSE...

...I KNEW YOUR *FATHER*.

YOU'RE *LYING*.

NO.

WE *WORKED* ... TOGETHER.

MAY I JOIN YOU?

IT SEEMS YOU ALREADY *HAVE.*

HAVE YOU BEEN *FOLLOWING* ME?

NO. *JACK* TOLD ME YOU'D BE HERE.

NOT TILL *TWELVE.* SHE TOLD ME *THAT,* TOO.

I *KNOW* YOU DON'T WANT TO TALK TO ME, ALEX, BUT WILL YOU AT LEAST *LISTEN?*

GO AWAY. I'M *MEETING* SOMEONE.

WE DIDN'T BELIEVE YOU, AND WE *SHOULD* HAVE. IT JUST SEEMED SO *INCREDIBLE.* WHO COULD HAVE THOUGHT DAMIAN CRAY WOULD *THREATEN* THE WORLD?

**ANTHONY HOROWITZ** is the author of the number one bestselling Alex Rider books and The Power of Five series. He has enjoyed huge success as a writer for both children and adults, most recently with the latest adventure in the Alex Rider series, RUSSIAN ROULETTE, and the highly acclaimed Sherlock Holmes novels, THE HOUSE OF SILK and MORIARTY. Anthony was also chosen by the Ian Fleming estate to write the new James Bond novel, TRIGGER MORTIS, which was published in September 2015. Anthony has won numerous awards, including the Bookseller Association/Nielsen Author of the Year Award, the Children's Book of the Year Award at the British Book Awards, and the Red House Children's Book Award. In 2014 Anthony was awarded an OBE for Services to Literature. He has also created and written many major television series, including INJUSTICE, COLLISION and the award-winning FOYLE'S WAR.

www.anthonyhorowitz.com

**ANTONY JOHNSTON,** who wrote the script for this book, is a veteran author of comics and graphic novels, from superheroes such as DAREDEVIL and WOLVERINE, to science-fiction adventures like WASTELAND and DEAD SPACE, and even thrillers such as THE COLDEST CITY and JULIUS. He also writes videogames, including many of the DEAD SPACE series, and other games like BINARY DOMAIN and XCOM. His debut fiction novel FRIGHTENING CURVES won an IPPY award for Best Horror. Antony lives in North-West England with his partner Marcia, his dogs Connor and Rosie, and far too many gadgets with apples printed on them.

www.antonyjohnston.com

The artwork in this graphic novel is the work of two artists, **KANAKO DAMERUM** and **YUZURU TAKASAKI,** who collaborate on every illustration. Although living on opposite sides of the globe, these Japanese sisters work seamlessly together via the Internet.

Living and working in Tokyo, **YUZURU** produced all the line work for these illustrations using traditional means. The quality of her draughtsmanship comes from years of honing her skills in the highly competitive world of manga.

**KANAKO** lives and works out of her studio in London. She managed and directed the project as well as colouring and rendering the artwork digitally using her wealth of knowledge in graphic design.

www.manga-media.com
www.thorogood.net

# Collect all the Alex Rider books

**STORMBREAKER**

Alex Rider – you're never too young to die…

**POINT BLANC**

High in the Alps, death waits for Alex Rider…

**SKELETON KEY**

Sharks. Assassins. Nuclear bombs. Alex Rider's in deep water.

**EAGLE STRIKE**

Alex Rider has 90 minutes to save the world.

**SCORPIA**

Once stung, twice as deadly. Alex Rider wants revenge.

**ARK ANGEL**

He's back – and this time there are no limits.

**SNAKEHEAD**

Alex Rider bites back…

**CROCODILE TEARS**

Alex Rider – in the jaws of death…

**SCORPIA RISING**

One bullet. One life. The end starts here.

**RUSSIAN ROULETTE**

Get your hands on the deadly prequel.

**alexrider.com**